Craftily EVER AFTER

#3

- - Tie-Dye Disaster - -

By Martha Maker   **Illustrated by Xindi Yan**

LITTLE SIMON

New York London Toronto Sydney New Delhi

This book is a work of fiction. Any references to historical events, real people,
or real places are used fictitiously. Other names, characters, places, and events are
products of the author's imagination, and any resemblance to actual events or places or
persons, living or dead, is entirely coincidental.

LITTLE SIMON

An imprint of Simon & Schuster Children's Publishing Division
1230 Avenue of the Americas, New York, New York 10020
First Little Simon paperback edition June 2018
Copyright © 2018 by Simon & Schuster, Inc.

For information about special discounts for bulk purchases, please contact Simon & Schuster
Special Sales at 1-866-506-1949 or business@simonandschuster.com.
The Simon & Schuster Speakers Bureau can bring authors to your live event.
For more information or to book an event contact the Simon & Schuster Speakers Bureau at
1-866-248-3049 or visit our website at www.simonspeakers.com.
Designed by Laura Roode
The text of this book was set in Caecilia.
Manufactured in the United States of America 0518 MTN
2 4 6 8 10 9 7 5 3 1
Library of Congress Cataloging-in-Publication Data
Names: Maker, Martha, author. | Yan, Xindi, illustrator.
Title: Tie-dye disaster / Martha Maker ; illustrated by Xindi Yan.
Description: First Little Simon paperback edition. | New York : Little Simon, 2018. |
Series: Craftily ever after ; #3 | Summary: Eight-year-old Maddie and her best friends are
inspired to turn old clothing from white and drab to bright and fab, but disaster ensues when
they accidentally tie-dye a shirt that belongs to a very important client of Maddie's mom's.
Identifiers: LCCN 2017060515 (print) | LCCN 2017046678 (eBook) | ISBN 9781534417298 (eBook) |
ISBN 9781534417274 (pbk) | ISBN 9781534417281 (hc)
Subjects: | CYAC: Tie dyeing—Fiction. | Best friends—Fiction. |
Friendship—Fiction. | BISAC: JUVENILE FICTION / Imagination & Play. |
JUVENILE FICTION / Social Issues / Friendship. | JUVENILE FICTION /
Readers / Chapter Books.Classification: LCC PZ7.1.M34687 (print) |
LCC PZ7.1.M34687 Ti 2018 (eBook) | DDC [Fic]—dc23
LC record available at https://lccn.loc.gov/2017060515

CONTENTS

The Call

Maddie Wilson's slippered feet swung back and forth under her bedroom desk. *Scratch, scratch* went her pencil. This dress had a sweet-heart neckline and feathers all over the skirt. Maddie got some of her best ideas first thing in the morning.

She was just adding the final touches to her latest design sketch when a familiar, mouthwatering smell reached her. "*Mmmmmmm!* Pancakes!"

Maddie ran downstairs. "Thanks so much, Mom! You make the best—"

"Sorry, kiddo," said Maddie's father, standing at the stove and

waving his spatula. "Your regular pancake maker is not available this morning. Luckily, she's not the only one who can flip a flapjack around here."

"Sorry, Dad!" said Maddie. "Where is Mom?"

"In her sewing studio. This is

a busy time of year, so she's been there since sunup. You should go say good morning. But first—get 'em while they're hot!" he said, handing her a plate. Maddie did not need to be told twice.

When she finished eating, she volunteered to bring breakfast to her mom.

"Thanks, sweetie," said Margie Wilson, looking up from her sewing machine. "Hey, do you have time to give me some feedback on my designs? I need someone with a critical eye and a passion for fashion."

"Sure!" said Maddie. It was fun to have a mom who was a seam-stress. Maddie thoughtfully stud-ied several pencil sketches with swatches of fabric taped to them. "Hmmm . . . that dress would look amazing if you added some sequins

to the hemline. And maybe using a brighter color, like coral, would make it pop—"

Just then Maddie's dad burst in, holding out a phone.

"It's him!" he whispered urgently.

Maddie's mom quickly grabbed the phone. There were a lot of "Yes, sirs" and "Thank you, sirs." Then, "Oh! So soon!" and finally, "You can count on me, sir."

She hung up and sank back in her chair.

"I still can't believe he hired me," she said.

"Who?" asked Maddie.

"Mayor Barnstable," explained Maddie's mom. "He asked me to create a custom-tailored suit for him to wear to the unveiling of the new town hall."

"Wow!" said Maddie. "That's huge."

"Huge and terrifying," said Maddie's mom. "I just learned that the big event is Saturday night. That's less than a week away!"

"You can do it, Mom!" Maddie said confidently. Suddenly, she had a thought: *Wow! This could make Mom famous! And if she gets famous . . . will that make me famous?*

CHapTeR 2

Some Colorful Inspiration

That night, Maddie drifted off to sleep still thinking about her mother's important new client. She wondered if mayors had red carpets, like movie stars. She pictured reporters and photographers begging the mayor for details about his fabulous outfit.

"My designer? Of course it's

Maddie and Margie Wilson. They're the best in town."

Maddie imagined boarding a private airplane with her mom, rushing off to help dress someone fabulous. What a team they'd be, traveling the world. And all the stars begging, "*Maddie, you must design for me. Please, Maddie! Maddie?*"

"Maddie?"

"Huh?" Maddie opened one eye.

"That must have been some dream," said her dad. He was standing in her bedroom doorway. "I've been calling your name for a while. It's time to get up for school."

Maddie arrived in class just as the bell rang. She slid into her seat and grinned at her best friends, Emily Adams, Bella Diaz, and Sam Sharma. Boy, was she excited to tell them about yesterday's big call!

But before Maddie could whisper her good news, their teacher,

Ms. Gibbons, cleared her throat to get the class's attention.

Guess I'll have to wait till recess, Maddie thought, disappointed.

"We're starting a new unit today," announced Ms. Gibbons. "The next decade we're going to study is, well, *groovy*, as they used to say. Welcome to the 1960s!"

She showed images, played music, and told the class about all the things that had changed in the course of just a few years.

"Politics, opinions, laws . . . music, too. A popular sixties song was about how 'the times, they are a-changing.' That was definitely true," she explained. "And the clothes changed a lot too—some of the styles, well, they were pretty out there."

The classroom exploded with laughter at some of the outrageous clothing Ms. Gibbons showed on the screen. Jeans with giant flared "bell" bottoms. Dresses in neon colors and crazy patterns. Jackets with wings of suede fringe and beaded peace signs. But

other fashion trends looked sur-
prisingly familiar.

"Hey!" said Cory. "I have a shirt
just like that!"

Ms. Gibbons smiled.
"That's tie-dye. It was
very popular in the
sixties."

"Cool!" said Maddie,
practically bouncing in

her seat. Ms. Gibbons's presentation had given her a great idea. Now she had *two* exciting things to tell her friends!

At recess, Maddie's friends were as impressed by her news as she hoped they would be.

"Are you going to meet the mayor? Can *we* meet the mayor?" asked Emily.

"Maybe," said Maddie. "Oh, and I have an idea for our next crafting project!" The four friends met regularly to do crafts at their craft clubhouse—otherwise known as the old shed they had fixed up in Bella's yard. "How about we tie-dye?"

"You know how to tie-dye?" asked Sam.

"Sure!" said Maddie. "My mom taught me. You just bind cloth with rubber bands or string and dip it into dye. Where the fabric is covered, the dye can't reach, so you get a pattern."

They all started talking excit-
edly, and soon it was decided:
They would each collect old white
clothing and fabric scraps at home
and meet at the clubhouse the next
day after school.

On the Hunt

"Today's your lucky day," said Emily's mom when she asked about possible items to tie-dye. "I was just weeding out some old things." She pointed to a pile of clothing. "Take whatever you'd like." Emily found two of her dad's old white T-shirts. One had a lot of holes, but the other was just right.

"Perfect!" she said.

Sam, however, quickly discovered a problem: His artistic family favored bright clothing. He could not find *anything* light-colored except . . .

"Can you tie-dye socks?" Sam asked.

"Maybe. You could also try this," said his dad, holding up a length of thick fabric. "It's an old painting drop cloth, so there's some paint on it, but I still think it could end up looking pretty cool."

"You mean *groovy*," Sam corrected his dad.

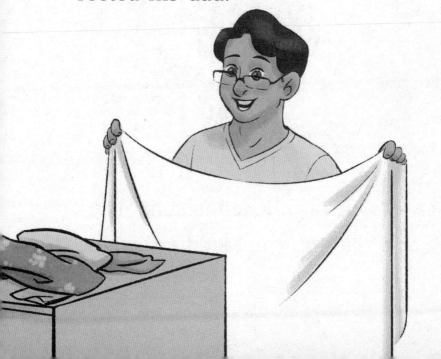

Maddie dug around in her closet until she found an old white dress. She had worn it almost every day last summer . . . until she had accidentally squirted ketchup all down the front mid–hot dog bite.

Maybe I can hide the stain under some colorful dye, Maddie thought.

She went to her mom's sewing room to get a second opinion. When Maddie explained her idea, her mom smiled.

"So resourceful," she said. "And so smart to recycle and refresh!"

"Speaking of fresh," said Maddie, "did you come up with a fresh idea for the mayor's outfit?"

"See for yourself." She pointed to her bulletin board.

"Oh," said Maddie, not sure what else to say. The sketch looked like . . . a basic, regular suit.

"I decided to go with a solid navy," continued her mom. "I think it will look really sharp in pictures."

Maddie knew that her mom had

a good point. And she did think the suit looked sharp. But she couldn't help feeling worried for her mom.

The suit might photograph well, but it was also pretty boring! There had to be some way to jazz it up. "What if you took some funky buttons and—"

"I'm sorry, honey," her mom interrupted, "but I just don't have the time to really fiddle around with things. I've already purchased everything I need, and with only four more days, time is of the essence!"

Maddie nodded. She didn't want to make her mom worry or slow her down. Margie Wilson already looked stressed enough!

"Looks awesome," Maddie finally said.

She felt a small pang of sadness that her mom didn't have time to

even hear her idea, but her mom
knew what was best. Right?

Maddie the Resourceful

The next day, the four friends met up at Bella's house. They went straight to the clubhouse and dumped their fabric finds on the big worktable.

"*Socks?*" Emily held one up, raising an eyebrow.

"And a drop cloth!" Sam added.

"I couldn't find anything," Bella apologized. "My parents donated a bunch of our old things right before we moved."

"It's okay," said Sam. "We can share my socks. I'll take the right one. You take the left!"

The friends laughed. Then Maddie got a better idea. "Hey, my mom has tons of extra fabric in her sewing studio! I'll run home and look while you guys set up."

After Maddie left, the others got to work. Emily gathered buckets, stirring sticks, and rubber bands. She also spread out newspapers to protect the worktable. Then Sam prepared the dye. "How about primary colors?" he asked. "Red, blue, and of course—"

"Yellow!" chorused Emily and Bella, giggling. It was Sam's favorite color.

Bella used her computer to research and print out an article on tie-dyeing that included instructions and designs. Spirals, bull's-eyes, stripes, rosettes—there were so many good options!

Meanwhile, Maddie arrived home and discovered that her mom was out running errands. She hesitated before going to the sewing studio.

Maybe I should wait until Mom comes back? she thought.

But then Maddie remembered what her mother had said about the tie-dye project in the first place: "So resourceful!" Maddie smiled, thinking of how fun it would be to surprise her mom by showing just how resourceful she could be. Besides, her mom had been so busy earlier. There was no way she would have time to help sort through scraps. Maddie had assisted in the sewing room so many times, she was sure she could figure out which odds and ends were up for grabs.

In a corner by the door, Maddie spied a shopping bag. Perfect! She grabbed the bag and quickly started filling it with fabric scraps. She also dumped her mom's rag basket out

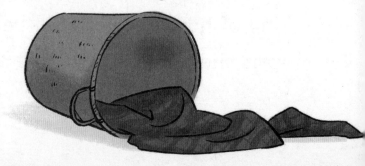

and found some old clothing items that she knew her mother would not mind her taking. She would return the bag and any scraps they didn't use later, but now she had plenty for Bella to choose from!

On her way out of the room, the drawing of the mayor's suit caught her eye.

Did he ask for a boring suit? she wondered. She really hoped so, because it looked like that was exactly what he was going to get.

"Oh good, you're back!" Sam said to Maddie. He and Emily were stirring buckets of dye. "Now all we need is—"

"Who ordered the salt?" sang Bella, returning from the kitchen.

"How did you know to add salt?" asked Maddie. Her mom had taught her that salt was the secret to making colors even brighter.

Bella pointed at the computer.

"Aha, I should have known!" said
Maddie.

The rest of the afternoon flew by as the four friends pinched and twisted fabric, wrapped and rewrapped rubber bands, and dipped and dunked their creations into buckets of dye. At first they stuck to the designs they had read about, but then they began to experiment. What would happen if they did a bunch of rosettes in a pattern, like a heart or a star? What if they did two spirals on the same piece of fabric, but in different spots? They also combined some of the colors of dye. Now they had green, orange, and purple, too!

That night at dinner, the phone rang. Maddie raised an eyebrow.

The Wilson family didn't usually get calls this late. But when Maddie's mom saw who was calling, she excused herself from the table, grabbed the phone, and stepped into the hall. Maddie could only hear snippets of the conversation.

"Okay, off-white, silk, French cuffs . . . ," she heard her mom say. "I feel like I saw it in the bag, but I

thought I had emptied it. . . . Yes, sir, I'll double-check, of course. And if you find it, your office can send it over anytime. . . . Thank you, sir!"

Maddie's mom hung up the phone and walked down the hall. When she returned to the kitchen a few minutes later, she looked puzzled.

"What was that all about?" asked Maddie's dad.

"Oh, the mayor has a special shirt he wants to wear with the suit I'm making. There's been a bit of a mix-up, though. His office was supposed to send it to me, but I just double-checked the sewing room and I don't have it. And, apparently, neither does he."

"Can't he just wear another shirt?" asked Maddie.

Her mom shrugged. "Of course, as long as it goes with the suit I'm making."

Maddie felt a stomach pang—and it had nothing to do with how hungry she was. She wanted to tell her mom what she really thought about the suit, but she couldn't think of a nice way to do it. Her mom always said, "If you can't say something nice, maybe you shouldn't say anything at all."

CHAPTER
5

The Magical Mystery Shirt

The next day, when school let out, Maddie and her friends couldn't get to the clubhouse fast enough. They had left all their creations tightly bound overnight so the colors could fully sink in. Now it was time for the big reveal.

First, Emily grabbed her dad's old T-shirt and snipped the rubber bands, being careful not to nip the fabric in the process. She unrolled it and . . .

Everybody gasped.

"Wow!" said Sam. "It's like a sunset, only brighter!"

Maddie unwrapped the stained dress next. It was now bright blue with purple rosettes forming a peace sign. The design completely hid the ketchup stain!

Then Bella unraveled a shirt that was more colorful than all the others. With its silky fabric, it looked like a shimmering rainbow.

"That one turned out so cool," said Maddie. "Who brought it?"

"Not me," said Emily. "I just brought the T-shirt."

"I just brought a drop cloth," said Sam.

"And socks! Don't forget the socks," joked Emily.

"There wasn't anything from my house," said Bella. "That's why you went home to get more stuff, remember?"

"It looks like a man's shirt," said Sam. "Maybe it's your dad's, Maddie?"

"I don't think so . . . ," said Maddie, trying to recall what she had brought. She had gathered up everything so fast, she wasn't entirely sure what ended up in the bag. It didn't look like something her dad would wear, though.

"Well, it's a magical mystery shirt, I guess," said Sam. "But I like it. If your dad doesn't claim it, I'll definitely wear it!"

The others laughed, including Maddie. Then Sam revealed his pair of mismatched tie-dyed socks, which made them laugh harder.

As Bella started to hang up the mystery shirt to dry, she noticed something. "Hey, a clue!" she said. "Look at the cuff."

The others followed her gaze.

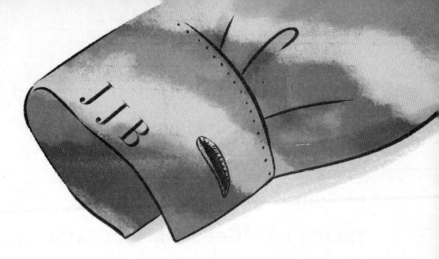

"'JJB,'" read Sam. "What is JJB?"

"You mean *who* is JJB," said Bella. "It's a monogram. Those are probably the initials of whoever owns this shirt."

"My dad's initials are RPW," said Maddie, "so it definitely isn't . . ."

Her voice trailed off as she suddenly had an awful thought. *Oh no. It couldn't be.*

"Bella, can you go online and do a search for Mayor Barnstable?" Maddie asked.

"Sure." Bella typed and clicked, then said, "Got it. Mayor James J. Barnstable's website. What do you want to know?"

"I couldn't . . . ," said Maddie. "I didn't . . ."

Her friends looked at her, confused. She almost couldn't say it.

"James J. Barnstable," she finally said. "JJB. I tie-dyed the mayor's shirt."

CHAPTER 6

How Do You
Un-Tie-Dye?

"What?" said Emily. "That's not possible."

"Why did you have the mayor's shirt?" asked Bella.

"His office sent it to my mom because she's designing that suit for him. It must have been in the shopping bag I grabbed. I thought it was empty!" Maddie was close to tears. "I didn't mean to take it. And I certainly didn't mean to tie-dye it!"

Emily patted Maddie on the back. "It was a mistake. It will be okay," she said.

"No, it won't," said Maddie. "Because it gets worse! This is the special shirt he was going to wear with his new suit for the big event. What am I going to do?"

"You mean what are we going to do?" said Sam. "We tie-dyed the shirt together, so we're going to fix it together."

"How?" asked Maddie. "You can't *un*-tie-dye a shirt."

"Are you sure?" asked Bella. "My dad's a chef, remember? I've seen a lot of food stains. There are all sorts of ways to get stains out of clothing, so why not dye?"

"Really?" asked Emily. "Like what?"

"Well, the worst stain was mole sauce. It's a Mexican sauce made with chili pepper and chocolate, so it was pretty bad."

"As bad as dye?" asked Maddie. "You may have been able to get chocolate out, but how are we going to get the dye out?"

"Let's see!" Bella turned her attention back to the computer screen. "Looks like one method we could try is using laundry detergent, baking soda, and white vinegar. I'm pretty sure we have everything we need."

Bella dashed over to her house and back again.

"Good news," she reported. "My

dad must really like vinegar. We had balsamic vinegar, red wine vinegar, cider vinegar . . . practically every vinegar under the sun, including *white* vinegar!" And with that, Bella plopped down a big glass bottle.

Bella sat back down at her computer to read the instructions. "Okay, you're supposed to soak the shirt in

vinegar," she said. "Then you make a paste out of baking soda and more vinegar and rub that on the stain. Then you wash the shirt with detergent and even *more* vinegar."

"Good thing it's a full bottle," said Emily.

The four friends carefully followed the instructions. When they
got to the final step, Maddie rinsed
the shirt with cold water until all
the bubbles were gone.

"Hey, I think it's working," said
Sam, pointing to the colored water
filling the sink.

"You do?" Maddie held up the
wet shirt.

She wished she could agree. The
colors might have faded a little, but
the shirt still looked like a rainbow.
Maddie leaned in to take a closer
look. "Ewww!" she said, recoiling in

horror. "Now it reeks of vinegar, too!"

"Okay, don't panic," said Emily. "Let's try something else. What if instead of trying to remove the colors, we added more color? That way at least it would be one color, not lots of them."

"We *could* . . . ," said Sam thought-fully. "But too many colors mixed together usually just makes brown. Do you think the suit your mom designed would look good with a brown shirt?" he asked Maddie.

Maddie groaned in response. *How can things have gotten so messed up?* she thought. Maddie might not have been a huge fan of the suit her mom designed, but she certainly didn't want to make it worse!

"Don't worry, Maddie," said Bella.

"We'll figure something out."

"Totally," agreed Emily.

Maddie nodded glumly. She hoped her friends were right.

They had to find a way out of this tie-dye disaster, and fast. The mayor's big event was only a few days away!

Looking for a Sign

At bedtime, Maddie turned out her light and tried to sleep. But in her head she saw herself holding up the shirt and seeing the horrified look on the mayor's face.

Poof! went the private plane. *Poof!* went the parties, the premieres, and Maddie's future as a famous fashion designer.

And what about her mom? What if the mayor was angry—like, *really* angry?

"You'll never work in this town again!" she heard him say to her mom. "You're out. You all have to go!"

"But—but—" sputtered Maddie. Her mom and dad were standing there with suitcases, so she knew there was nothing she could say.

She ran to tell Emily, Bella, and Sam. But as she did, they turned away. Clearly, they wanted nothing to do with her.

"I'm so sorry! Please don't make us move!" Maddie begged the mayor. "I like my friends. I like my town."

But the mayor wasn't listening. Or maybe he couldn't hear her? The

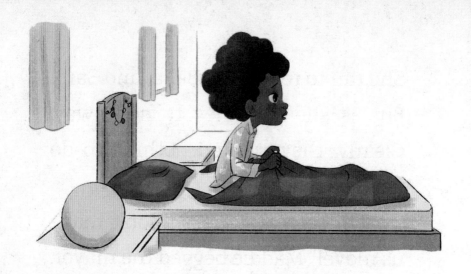

new town seemed really loud—

Maddie sat up abruptly. She looked around and then flopped back in relief. It had all been a bad dream: the mean mayor, the loud new town. *Maybe I even dreamed the part about the tie-dye disaster,* she thought hopefully. She got up and peeked into her backpack.

Nope, that part was real. In her backpack was a ziplock bag containing the damp 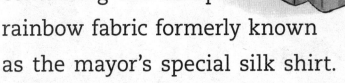 rainbow fabric formerly known as the mayor's special silk shirt.

The other thing from her dream that was real was the noise. Maddie went downstairs and found her father vacuuming and her mother cranking her favorite cleaning-the-house music.

Maddie's dad turned off the vacuum when he noticed Maddie. "Morning, sweetie."

"Sorry if we woke you," said Maddie's mom. "Just trying to get this place pulled together. We have a special visitor coming this afternoon: the mayor himself!"

On her way to school, Maddie was quiet. She kept trying to think of a way to tell her mom about the mayor's shirt. But every time she opened her mouth, she closed it again. Her mom was so excited to have such an important opportunity. How could Maddie ruin it?

At recess, Maddie quickly quizzed her friends on possible solutions.

"I looked online, and I even asked my dad. Don't worry—I didn't tell him why," said Bella. "But all I could find used bleach, which is a bad idea."

"Why?" asked Sam. "Bleach makes things white, right?"

"Yes," said Bella. "But it is also

strong enough to burn holes in delicate fabrics."

"Like a silk shirt," said Maddie glumly.

"I've been thinking about this," said Emily. "How about we go with you to tell your mom?" Sam and Bella both nodded.

Maddie smiled gratefully at her friends. "You guys are the best," she said. "But I was the one who made the mistake in the first place. I should probably be the one to take responsibility for it."

As the day went on, Maddie

tried hard to build up her confidence for the difficult task she faced. She looked for signs of support everywhere, and happily she found them. First, from her friends, who promised to come along if she changed her mind. Next, from the cafeteria, where her favorite lunch—pizza!— was being served, even though it was supposed to be meat loaf day.

Then she got her spelling test back. At the top of the page was "Great Job!" and a rainbow peace sign sticker. Rainbow, like the mayor's shirt, and peace. Maybe the mayor would be . . .

peaceful when he realized his outfit was ruined. Maddie was finally ready to tell her mom about the tie-dye disaster.

She *thought* she was ready. That is, until her dad brought her home from school. There were two unfamiliar cars in the driveway and another car parked in front of the house.

"Wow, looks like he's here already!" said Maddie's dad.

The mayor had arrived.

CHAPTER
8

Smells Like Disaster

Maddie wanted to run.

Maddie wanted to hide.

Maddie wanted to do anything but walk through her front door and meet the mayor.

But there was no way out. Before she could think of a plan or an excuse or anything, Maddie found herself in the entryway and her

mom saying, "Mr. Mayor, I'd like you to meet my husband, Robert, and our daughter, Maddie."

Maddie watched as her father shook hands with the mayor. Then he extended his hand to her. Maddie just stared.

"Maddie?" said her mom.

Maddie blinked and snapped herself out of it. The mayor smiled reassuringly as he shook her hand. "It's so great to meet you, Maddie. Your mom has been telling me that you are as good a designer as she is—which is saying a lot! She also says you're the most creative member of the family!"

"Would you like a photo with the mayor?" asked one of the official-looking people standing in Maddie's front hall. He motioned to a woman with a camera.

Maddie stood frozen, her backpack still on one shoulder, as the mayor got in position right next to Maddie. Her parents, standing behind the photographer, beamed, which made Maddie realize she wasn't even smiling.

"Thanks," the mayor said to

Maddie. "It is not often that I get to meet such a talented young art-ist like yourself." He pointed to her backpack. "Any chance you have any works of art in there I could see?"

"Oh, I, uh . . . ," stammered Maddie.

"Maddie, don't be shy," her mother said.

"She's always sketching out her ideas," said her dad.

"I mean, I . . ." Maddie unzipped her backpack slowly, hoping she'd quickly come across her drawing pad or something. But the moment she opened her bag, she regretted it.

"Whew!" said the mayor. He scrunched up his nose and stepped back quickly. "What is that powerful smell?"

"Oh no! I . . ." Maddie panicked. She dropped her backpack like a hot potato. It tipped over and out fell the bag with the rainbow shirt in it.

"Maddie, what on earth?" asked her father.

Her mother picked up the bag by one corner and sniffed it.

"It's . . . it's . . ." Maddie took a deep breath. A million possible answers ran through her head, but only one was right.

She summoned all her courage and looked the mayor in the eye.

"I'm so sorry, Mr. Mayor, sir," she said. "It's your shirt."

Feeling Groovy

Maddie couldn't bear to look at her mom. Instead she stared hard at the mayor's shoes. Suddenly, something strange happened. The mayor started to chuckle. When Maddie looked up, he had a funny look on his face that confused her.

The mayor seemed to be . . . smiling?

"May I see my shirt?" he asked.

Maddie nodded slowly. Her mom opened the plastic bag, removed the damp shirt, and held it up.

"Did you . . . tie-dye it?" the mayor asked.

Maddie nodded again, then closed her eyes tightly. She wanted to disappear.

The mayor started laughing even harder. "It's completely brilliant!" he said.

Maddie's eyes snapped open. "You *like* it?"

Now it was the mayor's turn to nod. "My dear," he said, "I am a

child of the 1960s. So naturally, I love tie-dye. Being the mayor, of course, I don't get to wear it every day. But it's not every day that we unveil the new town hall. It's a very special event and it deserves a very special shirt, don't you think?"

"Yes . . . sir," said Maddie, shocked.

"When I hired your mother, I knew she would find a way to wow me. My team told me she had a reputation for creating classic, elegant designs with an unexpected flair. Put this shirt together with the suit your mother has sewn and that's exactly what we'll have! A classic, elegant suit and a shirt with an unexpected flair!"

Maddie was still shocked. But she felt something else, too. She felt relief. Her mom wasn't going to lose her job! Maybe there would be private jets and celebrity clients in her future after all!

"Sir, I promise we'll have it

pressed and smelling fresh as roses by tomorrow," Maddie's mom said. "And I think I know the perfect way to tie it in with the rest of your outfit!"

After the mayor left, Maddie knew there was still one thing she had to do.

"Mom, I'm so sorry," she said. Then she explained every-thing: how she hadn't wanted Bella to feel left out. How she'd grabbed the empty shopping bag to carry the fabric scraps

and hadn't noticed the mayor's shirt at the bottom. How she and her friends had tried really, really hard to fix it.

When Maddie finished, she could tell that her mother was disappointed.

"I don't ever want you to take something from my sewing studio without permission again," said Mrs. Wilson. "Do you understand?"

"Yes, ma'am," said Maddie. And she meant it.

Then, to Maddie's surprise, her mother swept her into a big hug. It felt great, but Maddie had to ask, "What was that for?"

"For saving the day, sweetie," replied her mom.

"I saved the day?" Maddie asked.

"Yup." Her mom smiled and explained. "I worked hard on my design, and I am proud of it, but I kept feeling like there was something missing. Now I know exactly what it needed: you! I should have listened when you tried to help the other day."

Maddie couldn't believe it. She beamed with pride.

She was so excited to tell her friends how everything had worked out. But that would have to wait until school the next day. She and her mom still had important work to do!

After dinner, she joined her mom in the sewing studio. Maddie sewed a pocket square made from one of

the tie-dyed fabric scraps to match the mayor's radical shirt. Her mom put the finishing touches on what turned out to be an extremely elegant—and not at all boring—suit. She even added funky buttons sewn on with different-colored thread to tie everything together. Then they thoroughly washed the mayor's shirt (twice), pressed everything, and set it out on hangers.

Maddie and her mom stood back to admire their work.

"I must say, the outfit turned out perfect," said Mrs. Wilson. "The mayor is going to look really great."

"And really groovy," added Maddie with a smile.

CHAPTER 10

Making Headlines

A few days later, Maddie woke up to a familiar, delicious smell.

She grabbed her bathrobe and ran downstairs.

There was her mom, flipping the flapjacks. There was her dad, sitting at the table.

And there were her friends, Bella, Emily, and Sam, joining them for breakfast.

"Surprise!" said Maddie's dad. "We invited your friends over for a special celebration breakfast in honor of last night's success!"

"I brought homemade whipped cream!" said Bella.

"And chocolate syrup," added Sam.

"And sliced strawberries!" said Emily.

"Wait, *success?*" Maddie asked her mom. "You mean the mayor's gala went well? The outfit was a hit? Tell me everything!"

"See for yourself." Maddie's mom pointed to the newspaper.

"Wow!" said Maddie. "Look, it's the mayor in his new outfit! The one you made!"

"The one we all made," her mom corrected her, smiling at the kids around the table. Maddie had told her mom that even though the mistake of taking the mayor's shirt was all *hers*, the tie-dying—as well as the attempts to *fix* the tie-dye disaster—had been a team effort.

"And check *this* out," Maddie's dad said, pointing to the writing beneath the photo.

MAYOR BARNSTABLE CELEBRATES AT LAST NIGHT'S GALA FOR THE NEW TOWN HALL. HIS FESTIVE ENSEMBLE WAS CREATED BY LOCAL SEAMSTRESS MARGARET WILSON, WITH SPECIAL HELP FROM HER DAUGHTER, MADDIE WILSON.

How to Make . . .
A Tie-Dye Shirt

What you need:

Fabric dye
3-gallon enamel or stainless-steel containers
(You can use plastic, but it will get stained.)
1 cup of salt
Rubber bands
Tongs
Long-handled spoon
Fork
White cotton shirt or other
clothing item of your choice

Step 1:

In a container, mix
fabric dye according
to the instructions
on the package.

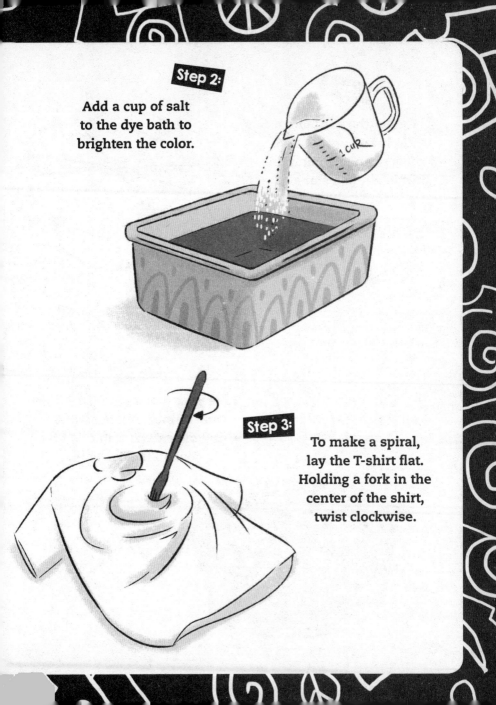

Step 2:

Add a cup of salt to the dye bath to brighten the color.

Step 3:

To make a spiral, lay the T-shirt flat. Holding a fork in the center of the shirt, twist clockwise.

Step 4:

Gather the shirt into a circle and wrap 4 to 6 rubber bands around the shirt in a rough star shape.

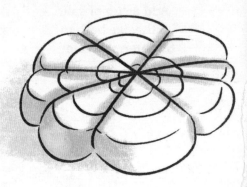

Step 5:

Take your rubber-banded T-shirt and immerse in hot water. Wring out excess water and then soak in the dye bath.

Step 6:

Stir frequently with a long-handled spoon for 10 to 30 minutes (depending on how deep a color you want).

Step 7: Remove shirt with tongs and rinse under warm water, followed by cooler water until the dye stops bleeding.

Step 8: Unwrap the T-shirt and line-dry. Ta-da! It's tie-dyed!

Here's a sneak peek at the next Craftily Ever After book!

Rrrrrrrrrrrrr . . . .

Bella Diaz stepped on the gas. The engine roared and the race car zoomed forward.

Beaming happily, Bella adjusted a knob on the dashboard. She had designed and programmed the race car herself! Bella loved all things about programming—computers, coding, and beyond. And she'd always dreamed of being able to program her very own race car!

She gripped the steering wheel with her purple leather racing gloves as she sped down the race track and into a tight turn.

Just then a light flashed red. *Warning! Warning!*

Oh no! She had taken the turn a little too fast. Bella spun the wheel, leaned hard and . . . *THUMP!*

Bella opened her eyes. She was on the floor next to her bed, twisted up in a tangle of blankets.

For a moment, she was completely confused. Then she realized what had happened.

Whew, what a dream! Her heart was still racing, thinking about flying around the track. And thinking about that amazing car.

She untangled herself and stood up. Glancing at her alarm clock, she saw that it wasn't even time to get ready for school.

Well, I might as well get up, thought Bella. *I could grab a few more minutes of sleep, but there's no way I'd have a dream that awesome again!*